To three men who love to cook
with kids: Nick Keyembe,
David Heckerling, and Salvatore Maccarone
—G.M.

Text copyright © 1994 by Grace Maccarone.
Illustrations copyright © 1994 by Emily Arnold McCully.
All rights reserved. Published by Scholastic Inc.
Printed in the U.S.A.

ISBN 0-439-45166-3

SCHOLASTIC, HELLO READER!, CARTWHEEL BOOKS, and associated logos and designs are trademarks and/or registered trademarks of Scholastic Inc.

17 16 15 14   40   0/14 13 12 11

Pizza Party!

by Grace Maccarone
Illustrated by Emily Arnold McCully

SCHOLASTIC INC.
New York   Toronto   London   Auckland   Sydney
Mexico City   New Delhi   Hong Kong   Buenos Aires

We scoop.
We pour.

We pour some more.

We fill.
We spill.

We wipe the floor.

We clean.

We fix.

We help to mix.

We push.

We poke.

We roll.

We joke.

We wait awhile.

We play.

We smile.

We pull.

We toss.

We stretch,

add sauce.

We cut.

We shred.

We taste.

We spread.

It cooks.
We look.

We read a book.

It's done.
What fun!

We eat our pie.

We're done!
What fun!

We say good-bye!